Praise for Paul Su

'In his latest collection [*Red Str*... status as one of Britain's most

—*Richard Keeble*
Professor of Journalism, University of Lincoln.

I was pleased to share these complex and rewarding journeys, and liked very much the worlds found or made here. Fine poems, to be sure. A mature and humane book.

—*Tim Neave, poet and scholar on Journeying*

'unique ...an unflinching and forensic exploration of a life through language.'

—*Jamie McGarry, poet, publisher. on New and Selected Poems*

it 'takes the reader on a journey which is both physical and spiritual.... I particularly like the notebook format which mixes short and long entries, prose and poetry. Immediate and sensitive observation of the landscape, its wildlife and small objects discovered in it are starting points for lyrical writing and impassioned meditation on central subjects.'

—*Myra Schneider, poet, on Spires and Minarets*

Paul Sutherland
Children, Routes & Red Streamers

Published in Ireland 2020 by Chaffinch Press
©Paul Sutherland 2020
All rights reserved
no part of this publication may be reproduced or transmitted without permission

ISBN 978-1-9161545-5-1

To all children desperate for home

Contents

A day trip to a primary school	9
A little girl by the lake *at Biyyam Kayal near Ponanni*	10
A traveller's vignette for Emma	12
The painted turtle	13
A passing teddy bear in the hands of a boy	14
A sort of kid ant-eater	15
'This time'	16
Animals she knows	17
Chalk	19
Spring's toddler	20
Grieving for Farrah	21
My granddaughter battles the sea with a red plastic spade	22
Drying coconuts	23
Rippling colours	24
For Ben on a rainy Christmas Eve	24
Among children	26
Papa and Grandma's place	28
Winter falls	30

Home birth	31
The mystic and child	33
Fractions of children	35
The invisible child	40
On trial	41
'Granddad' in family courtdefending his love of his granddaughter	42
Your grandma squeezed an empty dress	44
Hours leaving	45
Special children in care: the rainbow-spotter for Ross Darling	47
The party	48
On Kollam Beach	49
Afternoon in Meadow Park	50
Now you're nine —to my forcefully separated granddaughter	51
Smoke in our eyes	52
'The children...the children'	54
The funeral	56
Graves of the guileless	57
Unknown girl	58
Special children in care: Susie Tank	59
Strophe and anti-strophe	60
The velvet gown	62

Walking sticks	64
Foundlings	66
Buddleia and butterflies	67
The orphans' birds	68
from no Grimms, Andersen or Beatrix Potter	69
The sky-creator	70
Seven ways to approach grief	71
His questioners	73
Beauty and Bashō	74
A request from the background	76
Distances	77
from Seven Earth Odes, V, The Words	78
Random images of juvenilia	79
Small mosaic an address to the puerile	81
Red Streamers	83

A day trip to a primary school

In class, children lift and wave their
hands like reeds along each lowland road

the pupils colour words or draw balloons
around them and some desire to speak

one child voices a phrase making us tremble
who might give us a 'horrid cuddle'

some kids react with – a brother, cousin
a father – pain bursts from their writing books.

Once a dying novice asked 'what can I carry
across?' Y*our crushed heart,* replied the sage.

A little girl by the lake
at Biyyam Kayal near Ponanni

My guide notes, *there's not
a wrinkle on the lake*, I
peer at these aged hands

a white crane lights on
debris: a fisherman goes by
in his long narrow boat

the hanging foot-bridge
ripples – wishing to become
the water below

on the span, half-way,
I meet a girl – colourful
as a fanned peacock

'She doesn't act like
a Muslim'. My guide replies
her age, they're like this.

Her eyes stare up straight
seeking contact; each small step
reaching for salaams.

And leaving the place
she's there by our car with her
last wave through the glass.

My kind guide relates
Poets sing of this mirror
a face from its depths.

A traveller's vignette for Emma

I chanced to meet a five year old
who sought the scent of everything
picking off a petal she breathed

long and called herself a *winner*.
Of course she was never alone.
I gave into that aching empathy

for an exiled birth-giver and child
wanted to bow to their big hope
longing to be a companion.

On a straw she carried precious
drops from a small glass to a jug
and her fragile mother valued

each split second we could pool.
Emma wished to cleanse each thing
absorbed salt with a free tongue.

Her face's rosy chestnut eyes
must have dazzled me to silliness
I succumbed to each act of anarchy.

She railed *I will push you into River*.
From the bank, punched and shoved.
Against her little fury I lost my footing.

The painted turtle

loosening its neck
pokes a glamorous head
above the surface
with slow reflection
like a little girl
high-lighting
innocent
eye-brows and lips
in black and scarlet
to assist, into
the other world
her grandfather.

A passing teddy bear in the hands of a boy

The passing teddy bear is not a possession separate from the boy; it is the child. It doesn't represent the child. The brown fuzzy creature of portable size that the boy selects to carry is not a part of him or a sector or section, but exists in the boy's mind in a state of indivisible oneness with the boy, his carrier. 'Teddy' is a partner he can disappear into at will, to deflect danger or punishment and 'boy' can return to human self without friction because it is him, the boy, and the boy is it. To him, the walking male toddler, the 'it' is a universal 'you'. The relationship prevails beyond 'I and thou' because there is no distance between the inanimate object and the animate person for self-analysis to be attempted, an earlier condition to be overcome or a future to be worried about or hoped for. The inanimate teddy bear can never be removed from him to produce a forest of separation; the connection offers no splice between being and nothingness. Instead the mellow toy is an unfracturable entity that needs no eyes, windows, seam or soul; it exists without contradiction or conflict between the self and other.

A sort of kid ant-eater

A slick echidna wobbles away
into green by a gravel verge

wherever it goes a mysterious
soft snout confronts obstacles

its inventor thought first of armour
then shifted to infantile hope.

'This time'

'This time hide things so I can see them,' my granddaughter remarks – separating the idea of hiding things and the reality that hidden things should be out of view, if not hard to find. For my four and half year old, the intention of hiding is more important than hiding. It is enough to be playing a game involving the act of concealment than to achieve the objective. Her aim is mysterious but not unfathomable. She states her contradiction without irony or awareness of absurdity. For her, a view that hidden things should be or can be seeable is natural. She's surprised this reality needs to be pointed out – so she says 'this time'. The phrase admits the prospect that another time she may tolerate hidden objects vanishing. 'This time' she would like me to be sensible; not 'funny' as she likes to call me. I'm not convinced her excitement at finding things that are un-obscure is less than when she discovers things that have disappeared: her toys behind a cushion or inside a book, or buried under the toy box's clutter or resting beside a doll 'in ecstasy' where she would have expected nothing to be in that place. Her desire to find or unearth a thing never needs to be tested by ingenuity or conviction. That I can cause objects to vanish like a magician deserves little attention but that I'm engaged in playing the game influences her attitude – that all is well in her world.

Animals she knows
For Najia

Summer ascending
where the perfected moon pings
each white Zebra band

today she waves back
bush-leaves where a Fox might pass
shows 'her secret door'

from back of a tree
she leaps out and shocks with her
Leo's star-sign growl

'Beware of Guard Dog'
but whitest wands of Foxgloves
palisade the house

where suburb Sparrows
forget they've long been extinct
threading their chirrups

and Tiger Lilies
roar through a black wrought iron fence
after road-rage walks

where Gold Fish surface
and mutter their amazement
at being loved so much

she blows in my ears
a few remaining brain cells
jangle like wind chimes

this cul-de-sac child
who shakes many pink petals
on this grave-stone-head

then I'm a Camel
where no sand or oasis
ends desperate hope.

Chalk

Cypriot children mark with chalk a hop-scotch design on their kerb-less road. Two short, thick stalks of white rest by a gravelled verge. Two young sisters have been called inside for supper. Behind faded curtains with a floral motif, you can imagine their mother and father's delicious table spread. The daughters have recently arrived from school. Their pattern stays on the tarmac outside their grilled front door. Cars drive over their free-hand drawing. After hours, or maybe tomorrow, the offspring return and begin again their performance, hopping and stretching, tossing a marker and dancing ahead to that point. They sing made-up rhymes, competing with each other. If their one dimensional structure is washed into smeary wiggles or partially erased by the tyres of passing vehicles, they have two shoots of chalk to make the lines bold once more. Touching up their handiwork, the two girls' bare knees settle in the grit before a mutual friend peddles up and joins in. All changelings of Lefke belong in the match.

Spring's toddler

The morbid puddles
on the garden's furniture
dry up this morning

through the wood-slot fence
dividing this from that green
Forget-Me-Nots shiver

perhaps recalling
a granddaughter who often
offered life to death.

Grieving for Farrah

Black ink has dried on
a thousand and one poems
I might write to her

Slumping in prayer
I hug in my heart something
I don't understand

In the inner town
under speechless Orion -
who keeps on hooting?

Along the new-laid path
yesterday's slim ball-roller
hasn't left a trace

the red-finger-tipped
strawberry picker's vanished
among autumn leaves

teasing with her words
who played the *dungeon-er*
has locked herself away

My granddaughter battles the sea
with a red plastic spade

Dig deep, my daughter
on the shoreline where
sand is slick as a whale's tail
and hurl the water
back in each breaker's face.

Fight long and calm
without too much dancing
and giggling, bend to your task —
who knows if you will defeat
the waves or not.

Watch out, my daughter
the combers are tall as you
the sea may tumble you over
like driftwood, soak you
through - head to foot.

Be wise, my sweetheart
gather all the water you can
in your small spade's hollow —
who knows when the waves will flee
beyond the horizon.

Drying coconuts

Under full clotheslines criss-crossing a side yard, a vast number of old coconuts are spread, drying in Malabar warmth. I'm intrigued by the absence of grass; how the red earth supplies a background. Imagine troublemakers running, falling harder than on the lawns of my naiveté. I don't know, perhaps they bounce easily, are quicker on sandaled feet. The coconuts are split open so the white fruit dries and doesn't rot. Their halves look as if they should be catching hold of something descending with tireless sun rays, collecting what in a season will be harvested. At the moment whatever's being stored is invisible to my eyes. Someone will know. I hesitate to ask, valuing the certainty of not knowing. There are people more sensitive who see I'm observing and want to excite thoughts with knowledge. Another note: laughing juveniles, rushing from one house to another through un-fenced backyards, leave the coconuts alone. The coconuts are handle-less cups — large and tilted at different degrees, in an order-disorder that an artist might conceive. At separate slants, each hatch mark of the solar arc in progress will contribute to the final fruiting. Yet they appear too sensuous to be like calculators, cupping the passage of time. Love is in the mix, linking families and homes, easily connected whose facades look austere. The coconuts are an antithesis to builders leaning their dusty motorcycles against trees. Workers leave unfinished touches to new window sills and doors, likely never to be perfected. Coconut halves rest totally whole and absorb immeasurable changes, like a mother's heart turning to hug one infant and then feeling another maturing inside, in a territory with a big population in which each birth is invaluable.

Rippling colours

A stream of children
hold up placards for Child Day
walking a thin verge

their teachers frantic
watching no small one stumbles
Muslim or Hindu

safely arrived
kids, wiggle and chatter, wait
in the school hall.

For Ben on a rainy Christmas Eve

Benjamin longs for snow.
How else can Santa Claus
manoeuvre his sleigh?

Ben conjures that his duvet
stretched on the floor could furnish
a soft landing site

for *a miniature sleigh*
and eight tiny reindeers... with a little old
driver, so lively and quick... .

Rain clatters, wind whistles.
But imagine a fledgling boy
out-schemes the elements

and from the ledge of his bed
sees the night's shamanic visitor
who needs the love of a toddler.

Among children

*I — a white bearded tutor — visit a primary school
to teach pupils in an outdoor class creative writing
supposedly*

In summer-blue tops
Year Ones join round me and shout
'your chin's camouflaged!'

Ali, picking off
daisy petals, excites 'they
smell like lavender'

she yelps when a boy
speaks her nickname – I hope she
doesn't mind if I do

a butterfly weaves
each boy claiming it landed
on his finger first

daisy flower-heads
dismembered in 'he loves me
and he loves me not'

William taps his teeth
showing his 'Tornado hole'
whilst the rest sparkle

Jane insists she loves
the dentist 'I got 10 stars
to stick on my top'

their shadows stay close
to scabbed knees and bumped ankles,
bruised wrists and scraped arms.

Will some-day two imps
be lovers — recall the man
and Santa Claus beard?

Beau echoes 'but when
lost…you don't know who you are'
his little lips cringe

that Red Admiral
won't escape keeps shadowing
each round and thin face

to make this poem
I've pilfered words from children
whose day's never long

at night they will dream —
whether their homes serene or
torn apart daisies.

Papa and Grandma's place

In my imagination I arrive at Granddad's house, Papa's,
Grandma's, back in childhood, before I am ten, before
everything. A huge green veranda, street and dream-facing,
on which I may sit and scribble. A giant garden in the back
with fish pond and dove bird bath, two guardian trees with
thick trunks, a wooden bench between, near the lawn's end
and a compose heap in the south west corner. Inside, high
stairs reach to other homes – ours in pre-adolescent days.
Grandma's and Papa's is on the entrance floor, through twin
glass doors into a grand living space with a small statue
of Venus carved by him. He's in the cellar, down wooden
boards, space between each, I see through into darkness.
Then along a box-crowded damp tunnel, subterranean,
through no door into a room with tiny windows: one
looks out on the driveway, the other towards the garden.
Smell of glues. Papa's mouth full of tacks for upholstering
armchairs. Upstairs, Grandma's hands churn, flour-coated
with butter in a mixing bowl, making best cakes, Yorkshire
pudding on Sundays. Which territory to visit? Fragrance
of sweetened food in the vast kitchen, much light from
the garden from the west. Flowers in a vase. Downstairs
pungent, strips of tender wood being burnt by buzzing steel
saws. Oven heat in the light. Odour of shellac in the depths.
From Papa's workshop, what can I see? A small male,
in shorts, pre-school, post-school. What may I observe
of the garden? I try to gaze on all. Why can't I? Have to
be outside. Then looking in, can't discover anything in
the workshop or rangy kitchen. Can't peer inside, have
to bound indoors and go down to watch him with apron
and broom or upstairs, past the industrious range, past
grandma's apron and broom, and climb the quiet-sounding
zig-zagging stairs to our attic with small windows and
pointed ceilings – mum's and dad's and mine, then my

brother's too, then my sister's too, and then another sister until we move. Here the interior splits into two realities, nearby but different, one home ours, the other Papa's and Grandma's – separate places, not attached, three blocks apart. In a sense, dual father-mother-lands. Many houses, buildings and back yards stretch in between, fences to cross, hard alleys to sneak along, danger of meeting fist-clenched boys who smirk, 'We'll see you later!' I arrive at Papa's, Grandma's, under its green gables to the sky, at their dwelling perched on a slope, where visitors stay and lodge: a place of births. Past Papa's domed roses, I slip from my homeland, a teenage man, before their home becomes a place of deaths.

Winter falls

He arrived firstly guiltless and
played here, dreamt to slip-slide
across the roughen sheet, dared
to creep up so close to its ledge
to middle-stream with no branch
to cling to. River goddess smiled
through her open current's sparkle
but she cast-off, left him on the ice,
didn't take his feet and sweep him
snow-coated over her ceaselessly
fizzing lip. He returns, a traveller's
vista in his gaze, far less sturdy
afoot, observes again the fuming
descent then an evergreen gorge
shepherding its thaw-fed water
towards his remembered home
slowing between white moraine -
the thundering drop distancing
to one murmur. Against reason
the pain of someone disowned
seizes him as the melt swirls on.

Home birth
To Lucy Ann Hoyland

You came in the night
while I was baking a secret loaf
to rise with the sun.

It grew through dewfall.
Through the bedroom door I heard
your mum's gaping screams.

In the upstairs' bath-tub
saw soaking the bloodied sheets
of your late entry

I cuddled your slim form
but can't recall the moment
or your newborn eyes.

Your swaying oak crib
was draped in tame reds and blues
to soothe your homing.

I wanted to assist...
my hazel-nut bread was all
your mother fancied

scrubbing up loaf tins
in the sink, my ears cradled
your first small-mouth *whaws*.

In that old pancheon
the best dough I'd ever made
rose — your birth morning.

Fragrant as her scent
with each rich mouthful — your mum
must've guessed my longing.

The mystic and child

Under a single street-lamp, early evening, a Sufi engages with a girl child of about three, competing to see who has the greatest imagination. The dark curly-haired toddler drives a plastic wheel-based rocking horse. Its white wheels groan back and forth towards the lit house entrance or towards the lane's darkness. There is the common milling around of women outside the Sheikh's house. The girl's young mother is content with the Sufi approaching her daughter, a spirited horse-rider. Cars also half block the lane. She zooms towards or away, forward or back along rough tarmac. He points out her habit; she steers her horse sideways towards the cracked plaster walls of another dwelling, then spins her equine vehicle around, charging towards the road's other side where metal fence posts enclose the Sheikh's garden. The Sufi's first move is to stroke the horse's mane and admire the creature's features, its strong head and nose. She responds, stating the beast possesses a big nose. He calls them nostrils. In the semi-darkness child and man examine the qualities of the horse. He celebrates its eyes; she replies 'it has ears', gripping the handle she uses to control its wheeled gallop. He suggests her sturdy toy needs feeding. She cups her little hands under the horse's mouth. Perfumes exude from flowers. The mystic wonders if her horse might like to taste the night scents. She gestures that it is happy only gazing on blooms in the Sheikh's or holy man's garden.

With her vehicle-cum-horse the child stands, spiralling locks, in coat and woollen leggings; the temperature's dropped. Above, through little haze, stars emerge. The Sufi moots that maybe they could feed her horse stars; perhaps it would like that. The three-year old retorts 'no', and after a pause asserts, 'the sky's too high', implying her companion is an earthling. 'Too high' she points with her finger. The grown-up reacts that some equines have wings; the sky can't be too high. This rejoinder brings a gasp of apparent reflection, then she imitates the rhythmic sounds of her steed. Answers with her intimate understanding of her creature-toy's feelings. The Sufi listens, not convinced by her practiced whinnies. Staying silent in the darkness, he hopes to tease the child to further ingenuity. All at once, not in a logical jump, she binds their playfulness into a potent statement. Stretching an arm above her head towards the stars, she extols, 'They're all twinkling horses!' then waves a small hand across the span of the spotted cosmos. The mystic concedes that she is the imagination-master offering a make-believe bow.

Fractions of children

'these baby blue eyes
will not close on those who fear
our coming ashore'
　　　*
preparing our car
for scrap – we find a baby's
teeth-honed elephant
　　　*
such small steps tremor
through a hedgerow ditch
blooming with whiteness
　　　*
we request — two girl-
teenagers, each on a swing,
to pray for a child's freedom

they turn into gulls
circling as if they'll not
return to the sea.
　　　*
a red-jumper kid
harasses white-winged scroungers -
then pecks in the sand
　　　*
after playing deaf
to his sister's blaring bike bell
a brother responds
　　　*
A nest-less woman
with a five year-old
along a river damp trail
grows calm remembering
cockatoos… protect us.

                *
through Hajj millions
mutilated youngsters plea -
no fear being crushed

noon-stomping, a boy
Qur'an seller steers in place
his piled up wagon
                *
a life's down-turned eyes
the eternal summer floats
between nursing hands

softly clearing stains
a name appears on boyhood's
'no man's land' snare drum

shocked you discover
he was raised in your locale
died within your breath
                *
Now feel and ache
for the peace time's
abandoned – absorb
ferocious shivering
of little fuzzy arms,
hand fused in hand,
crossing wired frontiers,
tears sacks sagging,
nothing in their stomachs
dry lips cracking with screams…

20,000 orphans pour from one Islamic country into another. Faith works when the faithful behave from the toe tip to their head's hair, obey ancient obligations and connections that inspire and enlighten and give courage and engender mercy. We can prove those ways achieve in some individuals a blissful resistance to hatred, vanity, back-biting and the need for lies and secrets. But think of another child crusade and what hard masters those minors found and had to serve across killing fields. When children are orphaned, adults have failed.

*

we wait for someone
to walk out of a column
holding a baby
*
school kids tramping
the brink - dark brown hijabs
dark brown blazers
*
bare-foot, two toddlers
create a twilight track from
a long black settee
*
Our small grandchild says
'yellow' — giving up on books
in lemony fields

her mum pressing green
between both hands' forefingers
blows an eagle screel

if we climb too high
too far, border guards might shoot...
intending to miss.

   *

a pilgrim cradles
under desert thunderbolts
nursing her love-child
   *

Faith of some children
is more than the loud ocean
of doubts and deceits.

In traditional stories handed down to us, called fairy tales, departure is more than a natural progression towards independence or maturity. It represents an encounter with destructive forces of the world, which on the surface, a young person looks ill-equipped to tolerate. In critical episodes in some tales, a child-protagonist physically departs from his or her parents or other nourishing support (or is forcefully separated) and faces the universe alone or in shared solitude. The child is required to set its diminutive persona against the unknown's immense strength. And yet the child wins through, allowed to return to a sometimes transformed home. These tales show the resilience of children against upheavals in the adult world, overcoming conflicts between mother and father or the absence of loved ones. But a minor's innocence is not presented as the most potent catalyst. It is when the child is ready, desperate, to step from immunity into the clothing of knowledge and pain. In that meta-state, the leap in-between, at that moment, the young adventurer standing isolated carries insights to help defeat adult violence and trickery. Perhaps the narrated young have been prepared through many struggles with his or her progenitors and other grown-ups. The naive have tested the water and been tested. They are not war-mongers. The child has to survive our intimate and global wars.

*

A guy from Western Australia
at a Sydney midnight party said
My wife committed suicide —
I had the shotgun in my mouth
before I realised
only I could care for our daughter.

The invisible child

Night cleaners hadn't done their job; the court oozed revenge. Damp daylight reeked of the death of all things child-like and innocent. Occupants argued over a child's fate. How was that possible? Each angry participant had lost childhood in battles of separation, divorce, sat unforgiving to anyone who tried to rescue a youngster from estrangement and restore one fragment of happiness, origins, unity or sanity to the process of life, love and death.

Five fought their corners in a configuration of tables aligned to four sides of a puzzle. One in the oppositional place, another favoured, some in authority, decision-makers, another witness, a legal advisor, a shadow-observer who might go home afterwards and hug her children tightly or drink doses of cocoa. She hid behind a PC monitor, like the one in the favoured chair, the child's mum, a half-combatant supported by a stripy solicitor, never knowing if the Hearing will be a free-for-all, whether she'll have to defend her motherhood. No blood, dust or sawdust in the square ring, nothing depicting combat between love and hate, truth and fiction. A magic square held in the debate. Invisible, the child stood in the centre . Eight years, not a toddler, pleading for adults to behave, to care, to pardon each other. The child didn't favour revenge or want its ears burned by anyone.

On trial

I stood in that embittered room pining for justice
that some person would comprehend my cause —
if not of your blood — my feelings for you were just
and yours for me, a child, I an overgrown man.

In that hopeless chamber I trusted in sincerity
that some master would back-up our connection —
despite years estranged you longed to renew touch
with one who'd carried you from a cruel family.

Epochs of debate had earned you the right to speak
of surreal and playful visions and your missing love
to whisper into a judge's ears your distant wisdom

of peace – and yet in that blackish box those dreams
of sharing were dismembered by a coarser morality
and no one crouched to hear your blameless voice

A [family] court shall have regard particularly to
(a) the ascertainable wishes and feelings of the child
(considered in the light of age and understanding)

Children Act, 1989

'Granddad' in family court
defending his love of his granddaughter

'They set me in the adversarial chair
in a square corral of joined-up tables
no one bothered with soft nose mics.
You would've said *boring adult stuff*.
The three narrow — or was it huffy-faced
magistrates hummed to your seated mum
angled on the right; they teased this ordeal
should soon be done. She stiff and stylish
the best made, kept her doll shape to grey
however had on those tall heels just in case.
I'm not sure the girl in you liked dolls much
the way you used to hurl them to the ceiling.
Would I catch them? You laughed if I missed.
Standing by her, a sergeant major of a solicitor
in his pin-up-stripes and scarlet – would address
your birth-giver with my lady that, my lady this
as if a frustrated knight from King Arthur's court.
You might have been impressed with that poser.
Then it was my turn, the threesome said be brief
and tell us about your connection with the child
thumb-nailing unfathomable you. And I knew
I was a dead in the water if that relates to your
quacks quacks, I couldn't even flex my joints
to scramble to my feet and everything uttered
tumbled flat and someone's hands gesticulated
that couldn't have been mine. I tried to reveal
your art, a recondite poem you'd recited to me.
I guess you recall our once upon a time thrills.
I pointed to a photo of us at play, but for those
three flabby furies or cold rationalists — caring
only that you earned the best grades in school
¬uch fun images or made-up phrases sounded

almost creepy. So, a convict, I begged at last
that my connection with you was not bond
of someone's blood but more bond of love
and you should've seen their faces turn in
wrenched rage (and you won't be surprised
to learn) how they cursed me with an order
shot a glare and forced me to pay the cost.'

Your grandma squeezed an empty dress

She went to the sales at Monsoon. Given permission from your father to buy you an Eid dress, though he said in his manner, 'have no expectations'. He was bitter, having won the right to see you after a year and a half of forced separation. He was cautious, frightened to upset your mum, your primary carer. It was an excuse. You were eight years of age, far from your grandma, making you older, harder for her to know which apparel might suit your dreams. She left on the morning train, returning late afternoon. Summer, sticky shirted men leaped out ahead of her, then she appeared with a weighted bag. At home, she was hardly through the door when she reached in and pulled out your dress – a magician lifting a multi-coloured rabbit from a trilby. She did not know if she would see you again. Her pain for her estranged family, including your mum, her love for you and them, deepened that stretch down into the paper sack, the reverse of a silk hat. She didn't spread on the green settee your frock of many patterns in varied directions in red, blue and gold chequer designs. A dress to celebrate. She lifted it, letting it unfurl to a little girl's height. You embraced its fabric, filled out that garment, making it three dimensional and yours. Sensing other absences, she welcomed your return to her small home, lifting you off your feet. Suspended, against her chest, distant you.

Hours leaving

1.
Over deserted toys
Winter's Dragon fires out
erratic bursts of white

2.
hardly settling
you're out with soaked gloves
trying to slap up snowballs

3.
back and forth we sling them
not one round – splattering
under sodium bulbs

4.
faced with a slushy heap
you gesticulate 'Come on!
Let's make a snowman.'

5.
later the full moon
the ground reclines crispy white
under your boot-treads

6.
you don't go to bed
until past midnight – who knows
what dreams chime through you

7.
you're disappointed
come morning – a white
pancake left on the grass

8.
at noon we play chess
you unearth a toy dragon
to devour my pawn.

9.
twice your little face
with no fire for your wishing
stares into my face.

Special children in care: the rainbow-spotter
for Ross Darling

One afternoon among modest hills before the summits, twelve year old Ross stopped in the path. I, his carer, feared a demand that we return home. Instead he gazed a pointer into space, into gaps between clouds. A gentle rain fell among short intervals of sun beams. He kept looking with great intent towards something unseen. Encouraged I began to follow his sightline into the ether and saw nothing. Then he exclaimed, 'Look, a rainbow'. So energetic a voice from this faint, soft-faced, sapphire-eyed boy; I looked, but saw nothing. About five seconds later I observed his rain-bow, 'Noah's bow' as it might be imagined. He turned, gratified that I shared in his gaze. That was everything to Ross, to share, be together, to reach from one person to another joined in partnership, a community. Now out there on the margin of a near uninhabitable region, in the profile of the uplifted rock and earth, he offered in a moment his genius, unshakeable wisdom (or it might be insight) that enabled him to perceive a rainbow a number of seconds before me, before anyone, before an adult would've observed the arching promise of violets, greens and yellows. I puzzle still what a rainbow may express, expose, tell, five seconds ahead of my seeing. He carried a mystical certainty against his lost hopes of family, between his pat phrases, 'it's a crying shame' and 'silly cow'. I recall, that latish afternoon, before supper, the walk back to the residential home and feeling small beside a giant of perception who that night would likely soil his sleeping place again.

The party

After our *iftar*
soon mosque carpets strewn with chips
our kids go berserk

they've been hushed for hours
now with snack delights — burst like
fire-crackers with joy

how will some mothers
and fathers soothe, draw them home
perhaps with star-nets

doors slam and elders
come along to pick up flung
Styrofoam cases

a pink hijabed girl,
covered each inch, riots with
prayer-hatted boys

they will never sleep
this side of tomorrow's dawn
when back in the fast

let's imagine them
at one with the universe
teasing Muhammad
sallallahu alayhi wa salaam

On Kollam Beach

Standing on sand I watched, as twilit kids hoist kites
higher than imagined. The colourful stretched rectangles
shuddered with paper tails shimmying. Lines bowed and
extended towards disappearance. Kites climbed above
food booths which cast haloes into engulfing darkness.
A short afterglow, a respite, had passed. Fliers persisted,
running the shore's length. The moon urging light against
smog, kites soared above, skimming haze. Only half-
following, the boys could not see to where their created
things ascended. With fantastic skills, they had made
flimsy designs that towered above worlds. Space hushed:
no airliners, fighters; kites ruled, trembled, swooping until
regaining altitude. I sank into the sand from the pleasure
of observing. A hundred danced above the percussion of
pounding surf. The beach tilted against the Arabian Sea.
Signs in Hindi and English numbered deaths of bathers;
some had misread the undertow that hauled the earth into
chaotic water. The kite-displayers aimed aspirations toward
the night, not conquering Ocean. Yet those determined
youngsters, I guessed, would companion any who fenced
with waves. My disturbed senses embraced the kite-art.
The shaking acrobats, high above electric wires, echoed my
emotions. To an awed dreaminess, the kites turned into rapt
creatures — for the boys, a new sky full of fragile eagles.

Afternoon in Meadow Park
for an older Najia

Your finger-tips stirred
leaves to paradise patterns
fallen and floating

your shadow fell on
the water from where you
scaled a stubborn tree

we worked a long time
trying to decode two names
knifed into its trunk

you mentioned when small
that you were a Giant — who
could do anything

I said bark's design
is godly – you placed your palm
in each curve's recess.

On a bench was carved
light and shade but love always
neither could respond

I captured you posed
by a split bole – a sun-burst
predicting darkness

you crept and snapped off
in a garden of exiles
Asters for our night.

**Now you're nine —
to my forcefully separated granddaughter**

A black Hellebore bows its
flower-head in January light

when will my absence end, when
will I see you on your birthday?

What can I send to outwit your
mum, what to toss to her dogs?

I'll dispatch a gift of Hellebore —
each petal will speak for me.

Smoke in our eyes

Hours a bird of prey's
whirled round us – as if it can't
desert a promise

arm-holds of sticks for
a rock-born fire — you re-tell
first flights in the dark

white smoke in our eyes —
what are trees' bleared shapes saying
to us the banished?

A small campsite kid
puckers pearl lips and you kiss her
on her bronze forehead

so young but is she
before she can speak the words
tasting the feelings?

Perhaps you're her doll
she takes bites off each ration
of food and feeds you.

Some with toasting twigs —
each aches, each longs for ways home —
a half-log smoulders

between blackened greens
after a passing rainbow
our sun vanishes.

You mutter 'can't match
those I once found in books with -
stars I see above'.

'The children...the children'

Do we face up to horrors
around us when leaders
clatter their molars and
sharpen their tooth picks
for another invisible war?

In the Combat Stress ward
our heroes are de-hero-ised
one lowers his green trousers
to urinate on the news on T.V
ochre stream washes the eyes
of the commentator; another —
out of the freckled forearms of
a friendly nurse — smashes a tray
of mugs. They explode half-way
across the room, half-filled with tea.

My neighbour (he's out, he knows)
when talking about his invisible
war-terrors he reaches each stretch
over our wire fence between my
trellised plum and his rose bed
his voice halts at the same point
with 'the children... the children'.

I know he remembers how he felt
their brains tortured again, again.

Perhaps like a sickening lover
who keeps presenting bunches
of flowers to the wrong women
a nation only calls their soldiers
heroes when they definitely are not.

This could be a fact in any nation
in the world, not ours, it could be
the truth in any, not any, in ours.

One case enough to be recorded
in a lost city an older girl-child's
raped; when the heroes have had
enough sex, they slice off her head
and go outside, find a stray dog and
sever its furry head then they bring
that canine's snout and all and fix it
on the stump of the girl's body where
it slumped against her corner bed.

You told me this, my love
and that decapitated twitches
inside me and her beauty keeps
leaking blood like a slaughtered lamb
hung in a far field shed and someone
says 'we're done here, let's move off.'

My neighbour grieves
***What's left after us warriors leave?
The children….the children***

The funeral

Backbones bent, four children approach
and lob objects into a street-end fire.

Under the confusion of hacked boards
the crinkled low coals startle like jewels.

One, a boy, perhaps nine, struggles to toss
his paper crown; it flies too far or falls short.

Some fear his writhing cheeks and twitch.
Why does he stammer in front of the blaze?

Now each hollers into the tongues of light
desiring the red flames would speak back.

Graves of the guileless

Two friends ventured on through Bucharest's children-filled, blossom-filled parks. A sunny Eastertide, Good Friday, we turned into the city's necropolis. Soon twilight spread over its structures, narrowing each thoroughfare toward altered vanishing points. No chance to see more than a fraction of the inscriptions, as if knocking on numbered doors. I talked poetry, touched by your knowledge of Romanian poets — the died-young romantics — nationalists too.

In the revolution of 1989, politics became sacred. We watched many respondents in faith, a procession of cherubim and mothers with flowers and candles stepped up a parade of stone stairs into a little windowless house, a collective tomb for the fallen. They paid homage in the Cemetery of Heroes, remembering that many of the slaughtered had been fresh students at the university who had rushed from lamp-lit reading desks out on to the explosive streets, who went from gazing over project papers to encountering the rattling fire of machine guns that left on city walls, when bullets missed their targets, a crude artistry of thumb-sized holes.

In a post-revolutionary land, something has been achieved. We heard the juveniles whisper in their parade 'we'll keep our little victories and value our freedom to express visions'. Adults, alarmed by youthful idealism, are frightened of the cause that inspired adolescent freedom-fighters. Everyday reality struggles to fulfil their dreams and the dreams of those men and women hardly beyond childhood who were killed binding forever terror and innocence. They clashed with gun-slinging soldiers, most of them only boys.

Unknown girl

Turning seven your sprightly fingers
swiped one stem of pink Phlox from
the surrounds of a gentleman's garden.
My wife and I placed your gift in a table's
centre-piece vase; after you had left for
weeks and weeks it perfumed our cottage.

Gradually it turned to a petticoat's white.
Those petals surrendered both their colour
and scent, they tumbled, speckling the water
in a back window ledge's pint size glass.

But don't imagine we disremembered you –
in our cold home — no matter how old you grew.
The season shifted far on to black winter
and the gentleman never noticed your theft.

Special children in care: Susie Tank

Susie liked chocolate, not scoffing, nibbling. She, ten years old, left teeth marks in dark brown blooms in the bowl at birthdays and holidays. She wished for the thrill of goodies without gobbling. Centre-pieces were guarded by 'co-workers' as the carers called themselves. She didn't speak, giving a secretive quality to attacks. Her rigid frame belied the speed of actions or displays of disapproval. Attempts to teach or socialise had marginal effect. Her swiftness disturbed the ambience co-workers hoped would extend through the big house, a garden of perennials lining a path from the child-resistant gate. Indoors, Susie found corridors for her to curl into a ball and somersault in rage. Some feared she might scream off an edge and spin down stairs but she knew when to stop. After an exhibition, without vanity or coyness, she held her hands in two Vs over her brown eyes, reversing her hands so the palms stared out.

Susie's tour de force occurred when the community visited the ancestral home of William Wordsworth, Riyal Water, at Easter. Dancing daffodils flourished that had inspired Dorothy Wordsworth which her brother converted to poetry. By strollers with poetic airs visiting the famous estate, Susie leaped, a short, dark-haired tiger, into hosts of daffodils and began to devour yellow petals, stems and all. Before a carer intervened, the damage was dramatic; peaceful onlookers stood open-mouthed. A state Susie grasped. She didn't sniff at but wolfed down flowers, causing concern, but it was agreed her constitution was iron plated; no need to worry. The ethics of visiting a site of national interest had been shattered. Co-workers retired with the group to their minibus and drove back to where collective lunacy made sense. Maybe Susie's untamed absorptions reflected in a strange way the origins of poetry.

Strophe and anti-strophe

She noticed darkness
of water bound between roots
was shaped like a heart

you didn't

she saw a bubble
once blown from a ring, resting
on a new-formed leaf

you didn't

she plodded in mud
in low suede boots – under mud
then kicked murk at you

you didn't reply in kind

She ran her fingers
down through a mere's overflow
and said, *do the same.*

you stooped and did the same

*I live in Outer
London. I hate London.
It's so polluted.*

Hmmm, you said

She called crowded blooms
in a window sill basket
fairies playground

you stared wowed

She chanced to expose
red dot of a lady bird —
stroked it sleep-fully

you dreamed

You claimed 'these are daffs'
she bolted, *you may have yours
but I have my name.*

The velvet gown

Behind men dressed in traditional garb, women and
children hide among banana leaves and varied vegetation.
Except for a girl-child in a burgundy velvet long-sleeved
dress which touches and flows across the coarse turf. She
lingers round the men: engineers, dignitaries, officials,
spiritual brothers in customary white, some fresh faced,
others quietly anxious.

With a thin gold necklace, bangles circle her right arm and
a single gold band on her left. No hijab. She wears sandals;
hem of her gown ruffling over sparse wildflowers. I'm led
to a three foot pit. In the north-west corner a section has
been spaded out, slightly deeper, for a foundation stone. A
labourer displays a tray full of wet cement, with a trowel
set in, for me to grasp and place mortar in the deeper hole.
Handed a square piece of marble 4 inches thick, I place the
marble using the remains of the tray's contents to point in
around the red-brown block. The chief engineer joins me.
I'm asked to say a *du'a*. Then helped out by brothers far
from their homes. Some will help administrate the building
of the mountain spiritual retreat.

I see her purpose, traipsing among bureaucrats and visitors;
she hands out foil-wrapped chocolates. Glides like silk,
offering from her transparent bag more and more sweets.
Far from her mother and female family, I visualize standing
at the top of the site near its edge or drifting back into their
home below the road's narrow fringe. She continues. I'm
drawn into dialogue about aims of the project, captured
in smart phone photos. A reporter approaches with two
cameras hanging from straps across his pink shirt. At his
request I extend praise, encouragement and anticipation.
Should have honoured the benefactors. She sits on a

plastic chair, first row, near the end; drinks from a paper cup, coffee. When it's not wedged between her knees, she nibbles a huge sun, a yellow-red sweet-ball. Looks surprised anyone notices.

I don't know if her maroon gown's been bought or handed-down. Will it be her wedding dress in a few years? It appears big. I fail to recognise its status, can't discern difference between a garment entered many times and one newly acquired for immediate need.

Walking sticks

An eight year old plods through and around rock pools
with a walking stick, a screw-on top. His granddad's
sometimes its hollow filled, like gold coin, with vodka,
he says, when granddad needed uplifting on a long hike,
I guess over those in view contours that dive to ocean.
Mine, necessary for my age, has a pheasant head carved
with an orange beak handle, pastime of a local eccentric.
'Do you believe in God?' the boy asks. I say, Yes, I do.
'Can anyone live forever?' His query isn't empty to me.
I've pondered. This time offer, 'God's the exception'.
My stick braces as we scrabble over crests of Devonians.
Booming white blooms rise above their silvered ridges;
pushed by a cold northwest wind the water roars down
narrow channels bedded and shiny with slate sediments.
In stranded pools my companion pries up settled stones
with his ferrule-less stick and disturbs soft hermit crabs
that try to find another hiding cleft. Dropping his staff
he traps his prey, two-handed, and lifts it up in his palms
to an occasional nip. In an Atlantic drilled cave shaped
like a crushed funnel we halt and listen to the sea-groan.
From that rocky hearing-horn each wave reverberates.
I miss my foothold by a murky ditch. He asks 'you ok?'
My Oedipus third leg doesn't always keep me upright.
Reek of sea weed itches, where the tide an hour before
backed off to leave the shore glossed with slimy green.
Trying to dislodge barnacles with his old stick, he slips
and wins his own soaking. Undeterred he jumps up fast.
I'm unrelated to this pal for a day, he trusts and replies
to my call when he's gone behind a volcanic screen like a
series of armour plates on the centre of a dinosaur's back.
He would know which dinosaur and pronounce its name.
He lives with a strange dread. Voicing it, I claim it won't
happen. He believes he will die at twenty-one; 'the world

has' he avows '13 years to go'. Sees his death plotted in a
TV doomsday report. Speaks like he's older than me.
When a boy, I didn't feel his terror if media raved about
nuclear fallout; superpowers bent on mass destroying. For a
brief time we trade walking aids, with granddad's
I pick over heaved strata, he grips the bird headed rod.
'I'm named after Bob Dylan. Know the song 'A Hard
Rain's Goin' to Fall'? , I say Yes as if no one's changed.

Foundlings

The wind tugs hard at
a travellers' train of white clouds
above the wood-lot

into the distance
the narrow highway's broken
by noisy shadows

the wheat's green turquoise
whines away from joined alms houses
with a half-closed gate

abandoned children
dying, sometimes found solace
among buttercups

for unknown others
a sacred plot – their beliefs
soughing in the verge.

Buddleia and butterflies
to Farrah

Are quivering Buddleia blooms
attracting August Peacocks
and shiny Red Admirals
darker on the under-wings
and flighty Cabbage Whites —
their twinning disrupted?
Or are painted butterflies
falling frantic into swoons
on purple, puce and mauve
the nectar cones shrinking?
My small sweetheart, if you
were under fractured shade
with me, I wouldn't hesitate
to ask you to make sense of it.

The orphans' birds

At Ma'adin Academy, in the blistering light
young male orphans announce them, *love birds*
joined as if one, on separate perches, and hear
affectionate chirp chirping chirping trills.
They feed every green and yellow budgerigar,
if their light wings stop quivering long enough,
with screwed up foliage through the cage's wire
each opening smaller than an infant's finger.
The birds with a scissor action snip the green
close by the fig tree with its enveloping shade,
the boys though understand those fruiting branches
are no source for the love birds' nutritious leaves.

from no Grimms, Andersen or Beatrix Potter

He remembers a four year old
with Athena eyes
who didn't wish him to read
from a favourite book
at bed-time; at mid-day
demanded stories to emerge whole
from his thought-entangled head.

He's still unclear, when with sweeps
she painted a field-leaping horse
without a rider, if he should've set
a fiction on its golden back?

When she recited, dead fish were dead
and she'd never eat a thing from the dark ocean
should he have lured her with a sea narrative?
He let serpents stand for omens of goodness
journeys into black as footpaths toward light.

To his adventures'
slithery morals or disabled plotlines
she stared up from behind the divan
out from under the stairwell
urging another fantasy.

The sky-creator
for the anonymous

Over a back garden —
autumn Vs honking —
he asked 'what do you see?'
And she responded with
mountains of geese

Seven ways to approach grief

Each year, my continuing little one, I am drawn to your tree, a Bird Cherry. This season its leaves redden, full of vigour, vermillion, scarlet and crimson in unimaginable shades. They hang in un-normal calm. Day by day dangle, without being forced to spiral down. The wind continues faint and the sun stays warm, pushing past the equinox into autumn. I struggle to understand your cherry leaves, why they turn red before other trees around this enclosure.

Your branch remains. No one's pruned. Where I placed you years ago, it shines and angles from the trunk before thinning towards the tree's aura of twigs. I hoisted you onto that bough. You sat observing. I steadied your covered legs to ensure you did not tumble. You, excited, a ship's hand in a crow's nest surrounded by billowing sails, saw a vision of love. In the same breath, you counted leaves and hid behind them.

Friends chastise – I must accept my loss. They excuse your ruthless mother and father who insist they have the right to break any heart they choose. Yet cannot succeed except through lies and distortions. They separate you from me against your will. They know your will. You cried out. They silence you with cleverness and false telling. Does it shout red, ashamed how human creatures can act with no esteem for truth or compassion, making your tree blush?

This year rouge, past embarrassment, lingers to profoundest red. Their fall postponed, colour deepens. Tattered, pierced with slits, I might pray a gale strips the tree. Let it be a shattered glass mosaic, nothing but bare lead. I cannot sue for an end when you have left this foliage. Your naive touch transforms the tree to red, to tell me you were here and will be here again.

Things spiral beyond empathy. Gazing on leaves, which in other years might be scraps and threads, your tree disappears to become another. Those who watch or pass by and marvel also, put forth their claims. Your intimate leaves mildly surrender, reflecting other worlds, other bereavements and estrangements. Over grievance and hope, yours is a sign of all I do not grasp. To stand, your tree must take root in my inmost being before nostalgia or amnesia hews it down.

Night watcher: I'm stunned at the absence of the sunlight how quietly you retake your place on a bark gilded throne. A queen, for these moments, you are suspended, not subject to time and space, and can now loiter. No one's jealousy or deception can steal from you and me, where I let my hand settle where you once reposed and gazed round your kingdom among red leaves.

Yet, I regret to say, your labour must be to forget me and allow future teenage and adult years to encompass until you inhabit them like rarest garments and you live through fresh loves that already start to shape your heart and conscience. In dishevelled age, my work, you continuing little one, is to remember all that we never lived.

His questioners

Their bearded father called and said they would like
to ask questions. He was escorted into an ante-room.

They stood in a row, in half profile, by a panelled wall
about ten feet from where he lounged on a long settee.

Heat leaving the day, at last night's coolness came in.
— One so beautiful, one leaned so covered, one so quiet.

Only the first in the chain of three, the youngest spoke:
'What do you think of our land? Our faith? Our future?'

Modest enquirer: he responded with courtesy of a guest
who'd been served delightful food, honoured with gifts.

He pleasured in gestures of her faintly reddening face.
At once sensed each daughter's eyes inquired 'now

handsome visitor, which of us do you think the most
beautiful, and be certain your answer will seal your fate.'

Beauty and Bashō

On that warm September Sunday, the police searched
for David Evans, who may have sexually assaulted
and murdered a schoolgirl. They also hunted for Anna
Humphrey the missing teenager whom he may have killed.
Bashō with friends bounced into a pub and sat around
tables waiting for the afternoon's band, slurping battered
pudding filled with gravy. They ogled tabloid 'pin-ups'
burning holes in the news. The one woman in the group
offered no opinion on the weekend manhunts. But sneaked
to see what the men were studying. For a second Bashō
sitting close saw the sex object through her eyes.

At some point the troupe drifted from the pub smells into
the beer garden sheltered by sycamores and open to a back
street. They noticed a young, attractively dressed female sat
at a picnic table, swinging her long blue jeaned legs. None
moved to ask her to join them or went over to chat. She
didn't beg attention and kept glancing into the distance.

Andy, the barman, came out and asked the woman, 'What
are you doing?' Perhaps she was in the wrong place or had
been offensive. 'Just waiting a lift,' she replied, and added,
'Here it is.' She leapt up and with a soundless skip jumped
into a red, low to the ground sports car as if this was her
world and she never worried about being abducted.

When she'd gone, Andy turned to the group with a grin-
cum-frown and explained, 'That one's a right mean tart.
We don't want her type hanging around here.' Somehow,
they were guilty of encouraging her to loiter with intent.
Rubbing his hands on his apron, he went back inside to his
duties.

After the Sunday band had performed and gone off and his friends dispersed, Bashō stood, absorbed in thought, by a picnic table in the out-of-hours silence. He relived the circumstances, conscious the molester David (whoever he was) and the likely pretty Anna may never be found. The poet pulled from his pocket a memo book and scribbled

Ancient witnesses share with Beauty a full-leaf chatter.

A request from the background

After showering, he sat limp in a broad armchair
in a blossom-printed chamber. Here, legendary
white-sleeved masters had reposed and prayed for *dunya*
and for *akhira*. In that curtained alcove to the *madrassa*

an 18 year old asked him to write a poem whose speech
was unheard, whose brows were unseen, who he never met.
Tempted to over-imagine beauty, her stinging night eyes.
Or was she wounded, disabled, unable to show her face?

Opening a way through green floor-to-ceiling-drapes
a pacified eleven year old, with a smile, accustomed
to being his sister's messenger, brought out a simple
childish blue covered book, with his sibling's wish.

The visitor scribbled thoughts, impressions of the room,
its pinkness. Later, unhappy with the first attempt asked
for another chance. Without distrust or pride her brother
again gave up the bound floral motif pages that floated

into the old man's palms. This time, the boy showed
extending his finger – *on these two pages…* he ordered.
He knew English, perhaps she didn't. Sleepily the guest had
a second go communicating through gathering night.

> *our blossom time's short*
> *but some have hearts and minds that*
> *surpass its downfall*

Distances

Returning from the West, I went into my neighbour's home,
before mine and my mum's aging cuddle. In passionate
love, I walked straight into next door's living room. You
stood there, two years older than the eighteen year old me,
shocked to see your October deserter return, who'd fled
desire running to the other side of the country, posting long
letters about black swans in flight. You were dressed to go
out, your husband upstairs, I heard his leather shoes tramp
on the ceiling. You were static, that clear moment. I crossed
the floor without warning and plunged my hand down
the front V of your silken dark dress, past embroidered
neckline, down to where it had never been before, my hand
icy from crossing a snow-bound continent, through drifted
gaps in mountains, over prairies hardly undulating (five
meals in five thousand miles) and round moulded shores of
frozen lakes, until the train approached our city. I stepped
off right through your snow-free front door. Two months
later, I slammed it so furiously, glass panels shattered.
Nowhere left, I limped back to my mother's embrace.

from *Seven Earth Odes*, V, The Words

When yearning's exhausted
the mind rejects all inclination
but to recede into those precincts
where no mourners wail
gardens and woodlands which held the centre
and peacefully retreated.
Those who loved them ultimately
still happen to stumble across
the hidden serpentine tracks
among the trees, and since the gate-keeper's call is heard
so slightly gravitate toward home
minor edens where we belonged, where whoever
passed through left an affectionate shadow
across the continuous outlines of the earth.
Why, mother, would it hurt you to know
how many mothers there are?

Random images of juvenilia

silver chrysanthemum
'Boys and girls, come out to play
The moon doth shine as bright as day'
*

an Islamic child
turns Christian, chasing pigeons
in St. Helen's Square
*

The shiest child-tree
dressed-up in crinoline colours
peeps from one front bay.
*

Humpy-Dumpty frail —
youth-gangs scurry homewards
making such racket
*

Through lunar, solar
dawn's parti-light, a child hums
with a nearby owl.
*

the cataleptic one
making her sign of terror
yanks stamens from hearts
*

a strange stubbornness
grips. If he deserts his watch
who'll revive the moon?
*

indigo balloon in tow
down the cobbled lane
in a wheelchair, a boy
*

grooming his keyboard
a terse step-son might compose
such awesome legends
*

Weather-glazed and shy
mossy flanks, light and heavy
child-ridden horses.
*

on skateboards, darers
at the core of the polis
fly over new plinths.
*

Emperor's new clothes —
climate kids see through the false-
hoods we put on each day.
*

some chomp sea-side rock
immense as dinosaur bones
with dismissive glee
*

blinds half-furled
in scented palms the smallest book
of Emily Dickinson
*

a girl's cheek-glow
shies from a moving window
washed by rain
*

on the chalked up surface
her disregarded coat - loose-ruffed
with blood red shoes – gleams.
She, suffering endless hope
prays for her mum and dad
to be in love again.

Small mosaic
an address to the puerile

the one who loves the snow
doesn't see it fall

twin sparrows, puffed-up,
a handful of space between,
in pruning shadows

when peace finally come
who will know it

pink-whitish blushes
mid-barren viburnum bloom
i'm haunted by me

the candle burnt last night
for un-recalled loves

the neighbour's children
have cast seeds on the pavement
for a crippled bird

fate has so many rings
for the grieving to wear

i dread to feel what
you'll think years from now when you
realise all we could've

tended to but didn't...
left you our world more broken

Red Streamers

Red streamers
through thunder-black
a ship off Spurn Head

deserted tidal pools
can't conceal gems

across the Wash
the Montagu lifts
in imagination

ashen Flags rustle
among railway grass

on the year's
last Rose of Shannon
a hornet lands

a red touring boat
in cross-currents

along the quayside
empty-handed – survivors
gather and depart

a yellow cab burbles
through city panic

eerie silence –
the control tower
at J.F.K

racket of swallows
disturbs sleepers

across the night
spacious star-chains
no one's sorrow can undo

John Clare mutters on
past frightened elms to his Mary

Mona Lisa's frock
braided in gold
a new horizon

rain's collected
in the O of his name

an abandoned son
rearranges dust sheets
before the clearance

streetlights silhouette
Rapunzel's tower

by the Trent
weathered graffiti alters
names of sweethearts

from a sparkling dock
mute swans cruise by

white hem whipping:
off both shoulders
her purple string straps

even now – the trickster's
love-bites on Birch bark

generations in love:
round the tied cottage
winter Jasmine

umpteen petals
blush the water

behind a pillar –
round as a ball
a squirrel cowls

a red Fergie drags old teeth
across last year's stubble

at the boundary stone –
heaped sugar beet –
a February dawn

one by one
star-points fade

daylight –
above the viewing ground
open buds of rouge

lying by the hedge
a hardly born calf

in the milking yard
worn out socks wiggle
from yellow and blue pegs

on tiled pavement
Periwinkles of light

on an embankment
a pink tricycle
nearly submerged

Humber's moon dipping –
mirror shield of Perseus

through windscreens
parked-up lovers gazing –
let their hands explore

in bunny gear a girl
by kerb-side sparrows

O Shit she exclaims
in bridal regalia
at the shutter's click

a Greyhound traipses in –
its female driver winks

from yawning maple
a whippoorwill
cuts through the heat

bi-plane dragonflies whirl
about the playing field

Grand River –
a highway swerves between
wild Tiger Lilies

fireworks shower
the Canada Day street

Nanabozho's hill
shines
under welcoming snow

two blanketed mares
at the bare-rail fence

a signal's white arm
raised between
frost-delicate slopes

curls of white bells
catch the gentle fall

through turquoise mist
fenland Savoy
ready to be cropped

on freshly dried overalls
a wind's fragrance lingers

hint of Coltsfoot
from undulating sand
by Bamburgh

by St Cuthbert's cell
snow in bloom

a sacred lake bed
glaciers scoured —
no water can hide

a killing field a rambler says
random weedtips emerging

a star on her neck
found, she reports, *on entering
a sunless hut*

on rocky ground, recalls
same size for stoning

a refugee,
Ghassan, speaks his name
Palestine

many unspeakable nations
fatherlands.....motherlands

an asylum seeker
holds the hand-set –
an ocean shell

in the same candlelit room
a guitarist and drummer

two millennia
of persecution
in a student's song

Bridge at Mostar
re-arches the gorge

the night road raised:
a Whitby trawler hoots
increasing furrows

who knows what hour
Sand Martins returned

early moon-fall
against darkness
subtle guides appear

a mountain's stillness
a twilit Kestrel hovers

back in the city
a drying Blackbird spreads
skeletal wings

in the park, Foxgloves
stare down the junkies

a teenage waitress
clears tables
wiping with both hands

on her way home
a Screech Owl hunting

above her head
a red beam pulses
crossing the frontier

nine on the Richter Scale –
the Blue Mosque shakes

gathered gulls
across the Bosporus
screeching into night

bare-armed in the shelter
lined-up for a typhoid shot

schools closed
local 'yobs' help rescuers
dig for a barking dog

speechless... the bereaved
sailing home at midnight

in depleted lungs
dust from crumpled walls –
the end of an era

city lights extinguished
siren screams in each quarter

a minute's silence:
Black Backs
chase a winter plough

red streamers from a snow ball –
Chinese Lantern on the sill

the chip-shop owner
opens his morning door –
black turban in place

St Hugh's roundel shimmers
where the Luftwaffe missed

a fighter's vapour trail –
a New Years' Dragon –
disintegrating

in a cold, abandoned doorway
two teenage girls slug it out

ornate supple lines
a beautiful woman's neck –
steeple at Newark

night rain's granules
on a necklaced back

before her first patron
a hair-dresser preens
in polished glass

once more – making sure
her burning hair's perfect

a cracked mirror
a youth asks: *had a fight
with your reflection?*

Joe Cool stitched on jeans
he likes to play 'call the police'

a polite rag doll
coughing – a kid carries it
to the farthest seat

a loner slumps to view
sun rays and river fret

her Guide Dog
a woman pursues with shouts
tapping a long stick

nicknamed the *Bat Woman*
by scamps two doors down

stroking carnations
she breathes their fragrance
off her fingertips

a dove-man and poet
takes his final leave

at night someone
at the cemetery stop
always waits to board

lips smudge the glass
kissing an image

under an archway
Homer in his travel-bag –
3000-year-old story

so far hasn't forgotten
the cause of his setting-out

somebody feeds
her newly born – a red band
below the bow's name

along a Saxon towpath
strangers point the way

en route: stop and stare
sun beams take root –
a buttercup field

this *busy-bee* bus driver
won't stop his whistling

steam-whistle-loud
a geared up soldier yells
from the platform edge

beside him: a cellophane bonnet
not Sally Ann or Jane Austen

her wheel-chair boy
watches another trip and fall
claps and gazes off

one limping under sail
through metallic blue

dusk, a skewbald
trots in a ring: a wrestler
limbering up

St. Guthlac rode through here
on his way to Crowland

with arc lamps
guards hunt for a fugitive
where a boy drowned

a Reed Warbler's
sweet-harsh singing

tolling the hour
from out of the mist
a swinging tongue

September light
on a heron's neck

her veil eased aside
a widow and youth embrace:
an oar blade drifting

a greylag's eyelids close
as if bedroom blinds

already in love
cuddling down in their boat –
soft words bubble-up

the moulting past –
new quarrels begin

his and hers pillows
fluffed-up
on a hotel bed

a peacock butterfly
around Pyracantha

a shunned admirer
spots her reflection
among scarlet leaves

November Rose hips
along a Keep Out path

yet welcoming
the owner mouths *hello*
without a voice

on contaminated land
exiles in deep blue patches

a mirror-cushion
from Afghanistan – the sun
speckles the ceiling

ice sheets wrap a palace
and shacks of refugees

the far shore crimson –
a young skater hesitates
prior to crossing

the quarter moon
escorts her home.

Acknowledgements

Paul Sutherland's writing has appeared in countless anthologies, newspapers and periodicals

Specifically, in Children's Routes and Red Streamers

A little girl by the lake at Biyyam Kayal near Ponanni appeared in The High Window, 2019

Animals she knows appeared in Anthology, Dempsey & Windle, 2015

Grieving for Farrah appeared in Pop-up Anthology, Dempsey & Windle, 2013

The mystic and child first published in an earlier version in Servant of the Loving One, Beacon Books, 2020

some miniature poems in the sequences first published in A Sufi Novice in Shaykh Efendi's Realm, Dream Catcher Books, 2015 re-published as The Shaykh and the Novice, Pim House Publishing 2016

Unknown girl first published in The Blue Nib magazine, 2018

from No Grimms, Andersen or Beatrix Potter first published in Poetry New Zealand, issue 34, 2007, then in Journeying, Valley Press, 2012

from Seven Earth Odes, V, The Words, first published in Seven Earth Odes, Endpapers 2004, re-published in New and Selected Poems, Valley Press, 2017

Red streamers, first published in an English-Romanian bi-lingual collection, Edituro Pim Press, 2019